Whoo-oo Is It?

For the kids at
Shirley Moore School,

Whoo-oo love
to read!

Megan McDonald

1997

A RICHARD JACKSON BOOK

story by MEGAN McDONALD
pictures by S. D. SCHINDLER

Orchard Books · New York

Whoo-oo Is It?

Orchard Books, 95 Madison Avenue, New York, NY 10016

Manufactured in the United States of America. Printed by Barton Press, Inc. Bound by Horowitz/Rae.
Book design by Mina Greenstein. The text of this book is set in 16 point ITC Berkeley Old Style
Bold. The illustrations are pastel drawings on colored papers.

Hardcover 10 9 8 7 6 5 4 3 2 1
Paperback 10 9 8 7 6 5 4 3 2 1

Library of Congress Cataloging-in-Publication Data
McDonald, Megan. Whoo-oo is it? / story by Megan McDonald ; pictures by S. D. Schindler.   p.   cm.
"A Richard Jackson book"—Half t.p.
Summary: Mother Owl hears a mysterious noise in the night and tries to identify it.
ISBN 0-531-05974-X (tr.)   ISBN 0-531-08574-0 (lib. bdg.)   ISBN 0-531-07094-8 (pbk.)
[1. Owls—Fiction. 2. Sound—Fiction. 3. Night—Fiction.] I. Schindler, S. D., ill. II. Title.
PZ7.M478419Wh 1992 [E]—dc20 91-18494

For Ben, Rachel, Jordan, and Keara

—M.M.

For Edwin and Bettie,
whoo-oo always listened . . .

—S.D.S.

Mother Owl first heard the sound just before dark. A faint *whhh, whhh, whhhhh*, like a tickle of wind in the trees. *Whhh, whhh, whhhhh*, softer than a kitten scratching on the barn door.

She knew that sound. From somewhere. Where?

Twilight. A ribbon of pink paled the sky.
Fireflies flickered like candles. Chill air let her know.
Night.

Hu-whoo. Father Owl gone, in search of food.
Mother Owl blinked. Once. Twice. It was time
for her to stir now. Feathers tucked around her,
been keeping her eggs warm all day.

Whhh, whhh, whhhhh. There it was again.
No more than a whisper.

Grrrrr-ff, grrrrr-ff.
Was it a puppy barking, far away?

Mmrrowww, mmrrowwwww.
A kitten crying, gone astray?

She swiveled her head from side to side, looking.
Listening.

A mouse, scurrying across the barn floor?
Tch, tch, tch, tch, tch, tch, tch, tch, tch, tch, tch, tch.

The creaking and sighing of the old barn door?
Eeerrrrrrrrrrrrrrrr.

She flew silently from her nest in the loft,
soundlessly over the farm, a ghost owl
white against the black ink sky.

Could it be?
A snake, ssssssssssssssssssss, that only she could see?
A raccoon climbing up a tree? *Churrr, churrr.*

Mother Owl knew the dark, its sounds. What was
this secret?

The *whhoosh* of a dragonfly's wings in the dark?
A woodpecker tapping, *tat-a-tat-a-tat, tat-a-tat-a-tat,*
at a tree's bark?

Near or far? Far or near?
Kwa-kwa-hoooo. Kwa-kwa-hoooo.
Hu, hu, hu, hu, hu. Loud and fast. Father Owl.

All night long, Mother Owl circled the fields
and returned, out, over, away, and back.
Sweeping, swooping through the trees she searched,
then flew back to her eggs, her nest.
Wondering. Waiting.

A splinter of light, no more than a sliver,
filtered through the cracks in the old barn.
Bits of dust danced, floated in the first light,
then settled.

Kkkkkkkkk-rrrkk. The sound of dry twigs
being broken.
   Near, not far.

   Round and white, the first egg swayed, jostled,
tipped.
   Sh-h-h-h, the baby owl called to its mother
from inside the shell.

Clk-clk-clk, clk-clk-clk . . .

A crack! Fine as the vein of a new leaf. Then out, out, out it came, eyes closed, downy as milkweed.

Whhh, whhh, whhhhh

Grrrrr-ff, grrrrr-ff

Mmrrowww, mmrrowwww

Tch, tch, tch, tch, tch, tch, tch, tch, tch, tch, tch, tch

Eeerrrrrrrrrrrrrrr

Sssssssssssssssssss

Churrr, churrr

Whhoosh

Tat-a-tat-a-tat, tat-a-tat-a-tat

Kkkkkkkkk-rrrkk

Sh-h-h-h

Clk-clk-clk, clk-clk-clk

The sounds of her new nestling! Right there
all the time. *Clack-clack-clack!* Father Owl snapped
his beak, spread his wings. Watching.

Mother Owl dried her new baby, snuggled in closer
to keep it warm. Waiting. Four more eggs to hatch.

Dawn.